Scoop's Ups and Downs

Written by Jonathan Emmett

Illustrated by Alex Paterson

OXFORD
UNIVERSITY PRESS

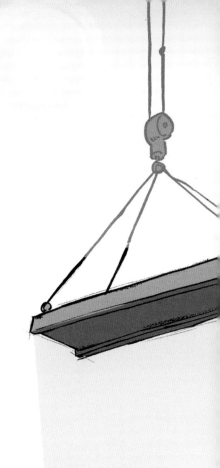

OXFORD
UNIVERSITY PRESS

Great Clarendon Street, Oxford, OX2 6DP, United Kingdom

Oxford University Press is a department of the University
of Oxford. It furthers the University's objective of excellence
in research, scholarship, and education by publishing
worldwide. Oxford is a registered trade mark of Oxford
University Press in the UK and in certain other countries

Text © Jonathan Emmett 2017
Illustrations © Alex Paterson 2017
Inside cover notes written by Teresa Heapy

The moral rights of the author have been asserted

First published 2017

British Library Cataloguing in Publication Data
Data available

ISBN: 978-0-19-841504-6

10 9 8 7 6 5 4 3 2 1

Paper used in the production of this book is a natural, recyclable product
made from wood grown in sustainable forests. The manufacturing process
conforms to the environmental regulations of the country of origin.

Printed in China by Golden Cup

Acknowledgements

Series Editor: Nikki Gamble

It was a hot morning in the town.

Scoop needed a cool drink of water.

4

He fell into the bucket with a **splash**.

The red bucket went down ...

... and the black bucket went up!

Scrap saw Scoop in the red bucket.

"Ha ha! You are stuck," she said.

But Scoop had a plan to trick Scrap.

"I am not stuck," said Scoop.
"I am just having a cool drink."

Scrap needed a cool drink as well.
So she went to the black bucket.

But Scrap was bigger than Scoop.
So Scrap's bucket went down ...

... and Scoop's bucket went back up!

"Thank you, Scrap," said Scoop, as he got out of his bucket.

"Now *you* are stuck," he said.

Scrap was in the bucket all morning.

Then a builder needed a bucket of water ...

... but he got a bucket of wet Scrap!